"Flora Jean &

By Nic

Arabella,
you
are
wonderfully
Made♥

Nicole
Penine

Dedicated to my Dad, there's never a day I don't miss our talks. I'm so glad you're not waiting around bored, wondering when I'm gonna get "Home" - I love you Bunches!

And to two of my brothers, Josh, and K-Bob. May you always be "brave," and your only pains ever only be "hockey hurts." Also, I'm the favorite.

Love, Nicc

Table of Contents

CHAPTER ONE

"Ten minutes 'till go time, Joys!" Mom shouted. "Last call let's get 'er done!"

Flora Jean Joy was in a tearing hurry. It was early on Sunday morning and she knew she still needed to brush her hair. She had already gotten dressed and brushed her teeth, but because she had been daydreaming over a catalog, she was now racing, pell-mell, through the hall into her mom's workspace.

She banged into the hallway wall and nearly tripped over the cat into Mrs. Joy's office area. Thankfully, she caught herself before she crashed into the worktable.

Mrs. Joy had no problem with the Joy children borrowing the hair accessories from the family business. But she would probably take exception to Flora unsettling the fancy display of hair-sticks, hair clips, and bobby pins. Mom was *extremely* particular about having all the hair pretties in their proper places.

With a twirl and pink-faced from her hurry, Flora twisted her slippery, copper-colored hair back. Then she took her favorite hair clip, a sparkly white snowflake, and thought about how she would wear her hair today. Making a goofy grin in the mirror, she pulled each side off the sides of

1

her hair away from her face, clipping it so it fell down in the back. Her Mom called this a 'half-up', her Dad (usually with a smirk) called it "business in the front, party in the back."

Satisfied with the way her hair looked, Flora bounced up and down a little to make sure her whole outfit was perfect. Today was an exciting day. The whole Joy family was going to church, just like they did every Sunday, but after the morning services they were planning to go to a birthday party for one of the kids in Flora and Fauna's Sunday School class.

Flora's twin sister, Fauna had already done her wavy blonde hair hours ago. She was perfectly dressed from head to toe and popped her head into the room.

"Florrie!" she said, excitedly. "Mom says not to forget our jeans."

"Jeans. Right." Flora cringed. "Why can't we just wear our leggings? They're so much more comfortable. And so much prettier too."

"Mom said that we'll bang our knees up so it's jeans or we can't go." Fauna replied. "The ice rink is going to be cold and hard."

It would be nice sometimes, Flora thought, *if Fauna would get annoyed at the same things that annoy me. She's just so proper all the time.*

"Okay." Flora said. She made sure her hair was straight, and she ran back to her bedroom to grab her jeans. Her sister Fauna quietly walked over to the couch to sit and wait for the rest of the family to go out the door. *We sure are different,* Thought Flora.

In fact, if you didn't know the Joy family, and met the three Joy sisters on the street, you wouldn't know that the children were related at all. Not only did they have very different personalities, but they also didn't even look like one another. *"It's like you all came from different shops!"* Mrs. Joy's friend Miss Katrina would tease. Mrs. Joy would chuckle and usually reply: *"We're so glad we have a variety!"*

Flora thought about this a bit more as she packed her jeans up. She started thinking about what sort of shop she might come from. *Probably a candy shop, the kind with rainbow jellybeans.* She was deep in thought over this when she realized that her Dad had been calling her over and over again.

Mr. Joy poked his head into the twins' bedroom.

"Flora-Bell," He said. "It's time to go, are you ready yet?" Flora nodded and ran up to give her dad a hug.

"Thanks Dad. I got so excited about Sadie's party, I forgot to listen for you."

Mr. Joy hugged Flora back.

"Just make sure you listen next time. It's your job to hear my voice." He tapped the catalog in Flora's hands. "I know you love skating and it's going to be a great day, but you need to focus on family stuff and try not to be distracted by these kinds of things."

"You got it, Boss." Flora quipped, echoing one of her favorite TV programs. "Do you think Sadie will like my hair? What if she doesn't like my outfit? Can I bring my skate catalog to church?"

Mr. Joy smiled. "Flora, I don't think she's invited us to look at our outfits and hair. I think she's invited us so that we can be friends and have fun together. The skate catalog can stay in the car. We don't need to be any more distracted than we are."

"Okay Dad." Flora said. She was still worried. "What if she doesn't like our present?"

Dad thought about it. "Well… it is a gift. My Grandad used to say, 'Never look a gift horse in the mouth.' so I guess since we're not gifting her a horse, we'll be okay."

Flora nodded. The Joy family had picked out a pretty notebook, pens, and a bobby pin to use as a bookmark the week before. It looked nice together. Flora just wasn't sure it was nice *enough.*

The Joy family piled into the van together and listened

to their favorite radio station on the way to church. Because Vespa was such a small town, with not many people, they chose to go to one of the neighboring towns to attend a church that had a larger congregation. The drive was about thirty minutes and the kids would always try to see how many different types of animals they could see on the way in.

"Cow!" Shouted Tansy.

"Horse!" Muttered Zeb. At eleven years old, he thought he was too old to play games in the car, but then again, to let his sisters win wasn't really an option. So he played things cool.

"Goat! Llama!" Shouted Fauna. "I get two! You only have one. Hey, Florrie? Are you playing?"

Flora looked up. She had been daydreaming about the ice rink. The Flying Y ice rink was the only ice rink in the whole valley. Any time that there was a chance to go ice skating, the Joy kids jumped for the opportunity.

Flora was reading her catalog and thinking about the last time she skated. She felt so elegant and peaceful on the ice. There were often other girls who would be in the center of the ice rink, skating in shapes or practicing jumps and special twirls with their coaches. Every time the Joy kids went to the rink, Flora tried to emulate the elegant, graceful movements. This time, she couldn't wait to see what she would learn next.

"I'm not playing this time. I'm thinking about skating." She looked over her catalog at her sister. "You can play without me."

CHAPTER TWO

Flora squirmed in her seat as the offering plate was passed. She sneaked a peek at the clock at the back of her Sunday School class. Only seven more minutes and the Joy family would be on their way to the ice rink.

She looked over at Sadie. Sadie was going to be turning nine. Flora and Fauna had just turned eight the previous month. They had gone out to a local peach orchard and had a 'peach party' with all the peaches they could pick, and an *al fresco* (or outside) lunch. It had been a hot, sticky day, but fun.

Flora fidgeted a bit more as she listened to the teacher.

"…and that's why it's always better to give than to receive."

Giving wasn't a problem, usually. It was the *getting* that was the issue. The Joy kids didn't receive a lot of spending money in an allowance, like some kids did. In fact, they usually only had spending money when they had a birthday or Christmas. Sometimes, they had special chores at home or at *Dusty Ranch* where they might earn money, but that was not very common. This hadn't really been a problem until recently, when Flora had found the skating magazine. Every Saturday evening, the Joy men (Dad and Zeb) had been going to the Youth Hockey Nights. Just last night, Flora had gotten to tag along and a lady there had given her this catalog to look at. It had the most beautiful things inside. Things that Flora knew would be crazy to even hope for. Everything in the catalog cost money. And money was short.

The bell rang for Sunday School to let out and Flora went with her twin sister to go find their parents.

"Florrie! Let's go talk to Juniper!" Fauna whispered.

Juniper was a new girl in class. She and her family had moved to town a few months ago. Flora and Fauna liked her a lot. She was the oldest of two children, had coffee-colored eyes, and a sparkling smile. She was very shy, so the twins walked right up to her and started chatting about the day's plans.

"I still can't believe you guys have an ice rink here." Juniper was saying. "It's the middle of the desert!"

Flora giggled. "Maybe they got too hot and thought that we needed to have somewhere to cool off."

Fauna grinned. "Or maybe they needed something for kids to do on their birthdays."

"Are you both really twins?" Juniper asked.

"Yes!" Flora and Fauna said, simultaneously.

"Flora is a minute older." Said Fauna.

"...and Fauna is a minute *taller*." said Flora. It was a family joke that had been passed around for years. They certainly didn't *look* like twins. Fauna had blonde hair, the color of corn silk, in soft, thick waves. She had green-blue eyes, and she was nearly as tall as their nine-year-old sister, Tansy.

Flora, on the other hand, had eyes the color of yellow amber, and hair the color of a copper penny. She had hair so slippery and fine that it often tangled and matted at the slightest action. In fact, before their family had discovered *The Purple Lady* this summer, Flora hadn't really done much with her hair. It never stayed put or held a style like one of her siblings' hair did. It usually just hanged in place.

When their family had discovered the *Purple Lady* at the market, with all her pretty hair accessories, all the Joy ladies had found that the special clips would hold their hair without a problem. Not only had the special clips held their hair in place, but Mrs. Joy had signed the whole family on to sell the pretty clips. Mr. Joy had called it an *investment*. So far, the family had sold the clips at a yard sale, and at a church fundraiser, it had been fun work and the family had enjoyed the profits.

"...and of course, we always get the cinnamon hot cocoa." Fauna was saying. "It's our favorite and tastes just like Christmas."

Flor found herself grinning at that reminder. The ice rink was such a special place to go. Maybe next year she and Fauna could have their birthday there.

"Did you have an ice rink in California?" Fauna asked.

"Oh, we had one, alright." Juniper replied. "We used to go all the time!"

"Juniper, let's go!" Juniper's Mom, Mrs. Lucas, was calling.

"See you there!" Said Flora.

The Joy kids changed clothes at church, then piled into the family van. Since the drive to the ice rink was almost an hour away, Mom had packed a lunch to enjoy on the way.

"Hey, thanks Mom!" Said Zeb. "I'm starving!"

"You're always starving!" Said Tansy. "Maybe you should slow down instead of running all the time."

"Nah," Zeb said. He flexed an arm. "I've got to keep my strength up. Besides! If I don't eat, I'll have trouble when it's my turn to play goalie."

Mr. Joy nodded from the front seat. "I was just like that as a boy. I remember one year, all I did was eat and sleep. I think I grew six inches!"

The Joy children laughed at this. Mr. Joy was very tall and adding six inches to his frame was something they had a hard time picturing.

"Actually,' he continued, "I wasn't sure your grandparents knew what to do with me. I certainly didn't get to go to *so many* birthday parties." He waggled his eyebrows. *"Work! Work!"*

Zeb groaned. "Yeah, but Dad? You lived on a dairy farm. We don't live on a farm. So there's less work, and more things to do that are fun."

"Still," Dad nodded, "All play and no work makes Zeb a dull boy."

On that note, the Joy family pulled into the parking lot of the *Flying Y Ice Rink.*

CHAPTER THREE

When the Joys arrived at the ice rink that afternoon, the rink was packed with families. Everyone from the Sunday School class was in the skate rental section getting ready to go onto the ice.

Zeb and Mr. Joy were renting hockey skates, these were shaped differently than the figure skates, with no *toe pick,* the part of the figure skate that allowed for the skater to tip forward and do special spins and foot movements on top of the ice.

There was a special room set out for the birthday girl and inside were Sadie and her parents Mr. and Mrs. Brown. The table was piled high with gifts. When the Joy girls peeked inside, they saw an enormous birthday cake covered in pink frosting.

"Ready?" Asked Sadie.

"We're ready!" Said Flora. She couldn't wait to get out onto the ice and feel the cold air and hear the crunch of her skates as they glided along the frozen rink.

Soon, the whole group was skating. Mr. Joy and Zeb had taken out their hockey gear and were practicing some starts and stops. They both loved to come out and play hockey. They would start skating forward, and then practice stopping with a T shaped stop, one skate making the top of the letter T directly behind the other skate. (This shape is also called *perpendicular,* which means that instead of two lines being side-by-side, they go opposite of one another, like in a plus shape, or a cross.)

Tansy was skating next to Mrs. Joy and laughing about something. Mrs. Joy wasn't comfortable on the ice. In fact, Mrs. Joy usually spent most of her time just trying to stay upright on the ice. She always reminded the kids: "Everyone has to have *something* they aren't great at. This is one thing that I don't do well."

Fauna was skating just ahead of Flora. She loved to go fast and soon was picking up speed, gliding and racing some of the other children on the ice. Flora thought being fast was fun but being *elegant* was even better. She took her time and practiced balancing on just one skate to try it out. She wobbled a little, but kept moving forward, slower than most of the bigger kids. She knew if she practiced enough, she would get better and better.

"Practice makes permanent." She said to nobody.

"Practice makes what?" Juniper was coming up beside Flora so quietly that Flora didn't hear her. Flora jumped a little but quickly regained her balance.

"Practice makes *permanent.* I know that most people say that practice makes *perfect,* but our music teacher, Mrs. Moody, always says *practice makes permanent.* I think it's because she wants us to practice the right way and not take shortcuts." Flora looked sideways at Juniper.

"That makes sense." Said Juniper. "Oh wow! Look over there!" She looked wistfully at the skaters who had just taken the ice. There were two teenagers and a little boy, and a grown-up who was dressed in a red jumpsuit The boy was spinning in tight circles, and the two teenagers were taking small jumps on the ice and practicing something that looked like they were running using the toe-picks.

The two girls watched for a few minutes together. Both caught up in the movements of the figure skaters. They watched one of the teenagers fall. It looked like it hurt.

"Hey, I just thought of something." Said Flora. "My mom always makes me put ice on something when I fall down. I guess if the figure skaters fall down, they could just sit on the ice and skip that part."

Juniper grinned. "Yeah, they could. But it's also really important to have your coach check up on you. Sometimes you can fall on the ice and get hurt, so getting things checked on by a grown-up can be important. If you are hurt and you skate on like a twisted ankle? It could mean that you get hurt worse."

Flora looked at Juniper. "Wow! You sure know a lot about skating! We've only been coming to skate out here for a few months. How do you know so much about it?"

"Well…" Juniper looked a little sad. "When we lived in California? we skated every week. It was one of our favorite family outings. But our parents decided we needed a change, so we moved here to Idaho. I miss it a lot. My coach said I was getting really good too."

"Maybe you can get a coach here!" said Flora. "Maybe you can find someone to teach you to be an even better skater. Can you coach *me?*"

Juniper looked at her new friend. "Maybe. We're still kind of getting used to everything. But…maybe. Here, let me show you how to do a jump."

With that, Juniper took a little skip, hop, and jump, before pushing ahead. Flora watched in surprise.

"Juniper, you're amazing!"

"Thanks." Juniper said, her face getting pink.

The two girls continued skating, practicing little hops and skips and balancing on one leg,

Soon the whistle was blown and the birthday group gathered for pink birthday cake and cinnamon hot cocoa.

15

They all sang *"Happy Birthday"* to Sadie and then watched closely as she opened her presents.

"Thank you, everyone!" Sadie said, when she was done. She had loved every gift that was given to her and was already tying her skates back on. All the kids chattered as they got ready to go back onto the ice.

Juniper nudged Flora. "Do you want to go to the pro-shop with me?"

Flora nodded. She waked over to Mr. Joy and asked him permission to walk to the little shop with her friend and he gave her some money.

"Just a small roll of hockey tape ought to work, Flora-bell." He said. *"No pink!"*

Flora giggled. She knew her dad wanted the tape to use on his hockey stick. The tape was used on the handle part of the stick, it helped his hands to hold the stick in place. Flora thought it would be funny to see her dad holding a pink-taped stick. Especially since the Youth Hockey Team was called *The Sharks*.

The two girls and Fauna went to the *pro-shop*. It was a little store inside the ice rink building. If you needed anything that wasn't food this was the place to be. The *pro* part of *pro shop* means *professional.* This is where the people who took skating seriously spent their money.

The shop was filled with all kinds of skating outfits, tools, and accessories. There was a wall that had all hockey sticks and another that had racks of outfits used to skate in competitions. The outfits looked like swimsuits with little skirts built in. There were all kinds of advertisements in the shop as well as more skate magazines like the one Flora had been looking at.

"Those sure are pretty!" said Fauna, pointing to the skating costumes along the wall.

"I think so too." Said Flora, she eyed a purple outfit with sparkles. "But they look like they would be *cold.* Plus, I don't love the idea of people watching me wearing a swimsuit. Why don't they have longer skirts?"

Juniper laughed. "Well, first, you get warm when you are skating hard enough. So, you don't really notice the cold after a while. And in a competition that is about being graceful, the judges need to see all the shapes, or *figures* that your whole body makes. It's a lot like a ballerina or a diver. It's not about being immodest, it's more like you're making art from head to toe." The Joy sisters listened to this intently. It made sense.

"That seems like something Mom would agree with." Fauna said. "She says that modesty (being careful with how you present yourself to others) is about the *heart.* Not so

17

much about what we wear. And that we should always dress for the event. You wouldn't want to wear something like that to church!"

"Even worse? Wearing a snowsuit to a pool could be a kind of immodesty." Said Flora. "I never really thought about that before. It's not really about what you have on, but *how and why* you wear it." She looked at the sparkly outfits one more time. "I guess we'd better get Dad's hockey tape."

As they waited in line to buy the hockey tape, (they were sure to get some *plain* hockey tape, not pink, though Flora and Fauna both agreed that maybe some pink tape would be a fun gift for Dad's birthday), they watched the owner, Mr. Stuart, sharpen some skates. He had a machine with a wheel that would spin quickly. As the wheel would spin he would take a pair of skates and push the blade against the wheel. It made a loud *whirring* noise, and there were sparks that flew up into the air. If skates weren't sharp, they weren't as safe to skate with.

The girls paid for the tape and took a minute to look at the Community Billboard. This was a board made of cork that anyone could put notes on. There were advertisements for events, coaches, used gear, even a notice that a little girl had lost her favorite stuffed koala, George.

"Poor George. I wonder where he went? Hey! Wow!" Said Flora. She pointed to one of the papers. *"Blue skates, size 2."*

There was a picture. The figure skates were gorgeous. They had bright sky-blue leather and some printed silver snowflakes all over them. She read the paper again. "$100 OBO. Call 555-5555. Wow. I saw a pair just like this in my skating magazine!"

"What does *oboe* mean?" Asked Fauna.

"I'm not sure," said Juniper.

"Well I'm going to find out!" Said Flora. Those skates were meant to be hers. Somehow, she would find a way.

CHAPTER FOUR

"One hundred dollars?" Dad repeated looking at the scrap of paper in his hands. It was Monday morning, Flora nodded over her pancakes. She had been waiting since the day before to ask her parents about the pretty blue skates.

"The sign said one hundred dollars, *oboe*. That's the number it said to call." Flora said, wrinkling her nose. "I'm not really sure what *oboe* means, but I *love* the skates, Dad. They're *perfect*. And they're *way* less expensive than the same ones in my catalog."

Dad smiled. "The sign didn't say *oboe*, that's the name of a musical instrument. The sign said Oh, Bee. Oh, that is shorthand for *or best offer.*"

"So maybe they would take *less* money for the skates?" She looked over at her sisters. This was even better. "May I be excused? I want to go count my birthday money."

She was excused from the table, cleared her plate, rinsed it, and put it into the dishwasher. Then, she ran as fast as she could to her piggy bank. She jumped onto her bed, avoiding Sulky their cat, and counted the money inside. She counted it twice, just to be sure she got it all.

Then discouraged, she slowly went back to the table where her parents were still sitting, enjoying their coffee. She flopped down and sighed.

"Do you think they will sell the skates for *ten* dollars?" she asked.

Mom and Dad looked at one another. Dad raised an eyebrow.

Mom spoke, finally. "No, I don't think that's a fair offer. You don't ask someone to sell something valuable for such a small amount. It's okay to make a *lower* offer, but because we care more about the person, rather than the thing, we always try to make a *fair* offer. I would say you need to have at least eighty dollars before you make an offer."

Flora frowned. This was not going like she planned. She wanted those skates. She thought they would look so perfect on her feet.

"Can I borrow some money? I really *need* these skates, Dad." She batted her eyes and gave her best smile.

Dad frowned. "A loan? No, I don't think that's a good idea. First of all, these are a want, not a need. Secondly, it's a bad plan to ask for money that you haven't earned. Money doesn't grow on trees."

Zeb walked into the room. He had his basketball and was waiting for the Franzosos to come over. Since it was

Monday, the plan was for the two families to do a science project together, eat lunch, then play until dinner. It wasn't exactly like a *co-op* (a special class for homeschool kids that meets and learns a subject together), but it was close.

"Flora, if you want to earn some money, I've got a dollar. You can clean my room." He said, generously.

Flora thought about her brother's room. She didn't like the thought. Her brother's room smelled like stinky hockey skates. He had a bad habit of leaving his socks on the floor too. A dollar seemed like not enough money for having to pinch her nose the whole time she cleaned.

"Thanks Zeb. I'll think about it." Flora said. She didn't want to say no until she had a better plan. She thought of something else.

"Dad, Mom? Do you have an idea of how I can earn that money? Not a loan, but…maybe I can do my chores really well and you can pay me for that?" She was hopeful.

Dad chuckled. "No, we don't pay you kids to do chores. Nice try, though. You need to do chores because you are a part of this family. If you don't learn to help out as a part of Team Joy, then it means more work for everyone."

Flora sighed. Money was complicated.

"I have an idea," Mom said. "How about you *invest* your ten dollars and use it to make some money."

22

"Remind me what that means again?" Flora said.

"You buy some bobby pins from me and get them at a *wholesale* price- that means you don't pay the full price or *retail.* Then you take the bobby pins and sell them to your friends at the *retail* or *full* price. The amount you spend to start is called the *investment."*

"Can you show me on paper?" Flora asked. "I think I understand, but I'm not sure yet."

Mom took a pen and paper and wrote out the math for Flora to see.

Bobby Pins Cost $1.00

Bobby Pins Sell $3.00

Total Made $2.00 per Bobby Pin Sold.

"Oh. That makes sense." Said Flora. "But I only have ten dollars to spend on bobby pins. So, even if I sell all the bobby pins? I'll be spending ten dollars to make an extra twenty dollars. But I need seventy dollars for the skates."

Mom nodded. "Let's see how your first investment turns out. If it works, we can do it again, each time investing a little more and selling a little more until you reach your goal."

Flora thought about it. "Well, can I have a loan to buy a lot of bobby pins? That would be much faster."

Dad shook his head. "No, that's another bad habit to get into. You don't know yet if you can sell ten bobby pins. It's better to keep out of debt and to save up for bigger investments."

"Okay, boss! I guess I'm in business!" Flora said, grinning. "How do I get started?"

CHAPTER FIVE

Flora and her parents worked together on the Blue Ice Skates Plan. The very first thing they did was to call the owner of the beautiful blue skates to see if the owner would sell them to Flora for eighty dollars instead of a hundred dollars.

The lady on the phone told Mr. and Mrs. Joy that they would sell the skates to Flora for eighty dollars and that she wished Flora luck in her new business. This made Flora very excited. She had exactly fourteen days to come up with the extra money. She carefully clipped the photo of the skates out of her catalog and glued it into her notebook for safekeeping.

Next, she sat down with her mom to figure out where she was going to find customers, which bobby pins she was going to sell, and how she would sell them. Knowing she only had a short amount of time to choose her bobby pins, she decided to go with what she loved best: five silver bobby pins with an *iridescent* (meaning sparkly) snowflake on the end, and five bobby pins with a delicate gold flower on the end.

Before she knew what she was doing, Flora was on

the phone talking to Mr. Stuart from the pro-shop at the ice rink.

"Hello, Mr. Stuart. This is Flora Jean Joy from church."

"Well hello! How can I help you today Miss Joy?"

"I am trying to earn money to pay for a set of ice skates, Mr. Stuart. Would it be okay if I set up a table to sell bobby pins to ladies who come to the hockey rink?" Flora paused. She hoped Mr. Stuart would say yes.

"That's an idea." Said Mr. Stuart. "Why not? Just make sure your Mom or Dad are at the rink and I can't see any reason why not."

"Thank you so much!" Flora grinned over the phone. "Have a great day! See you soon!"

The plan was set. Flora would set up a table in front of the ice rink pro-shop and would sell the gold flower bobby pins and the silver snowflake bobby pins to the ladies who came to the ice rink while the Youth Hockey League met. It was a great plan.

Carefully, she made a sign to put next to the table. The sign was white with purple letters. It said *"Flora's Fancies"* on it. She made sure to check the dictionary so the words would be spelled correctly. Mom and Dad were always talking about how important it was to do your best work in everything. Dad always said, "E*ven if things don't* turn out as you like? You can say you did your very best. It's better to try and fail than to look back and wonder if you could have tried harder."

The coming weekend was a special Youth Hockey Tournament. The event was Thursday, Friday, and Saturday nights. Mr. Joy had even gotten some time off special so he could participate. That meant that Flora had exactly two days to practice selling bobby pins. She made a list of people to practice on:

Granny and Grandad Rice

Dad

Mom

Fauna

Tansy

Zeb

Juniper

Franzosos

Sadie

The list was a good one. Flora decided she would make her phone calls tomorrow and get everyone in on the plan to help her practice her sales.

Soon it was dinner time and Mrs. Joy was calling for everyone to wash up. Spaghetti, meatballs, and garlic bread were all laid out on the table. It smelled amazing. Flora had worked so hard and been thinking so much, she didn't even realize that she was hungry. She filled her plate and gave thanks. It was good to be working on a plan. Those skates were nearly hers!

CHAPTER SIX

"Come and get your bobbies here!" Flora smiled. "Beautiful bobby pins! Get 'em while they're hot!" It was Thursday night and Flora had been at the ice rink, outside the pro-shop for about an hour. She rubbed her hands together. Even though she hadn't sold a single bobby pin yet, she was excited to be at the rink and just knew people would be buying her pretty pins.

Soon an older lady in a pink coat came by. She looked at Flora and smiled. Then she looked at the bobby pins and walked away. Flora smiled and wondered why the pink lady didn't stop. She was sitting in her chair, smiling. She had made sure that her sign was where people could see the words "*Flora's Fancies.*"

Mr. Stuart walked by. He turned to Flora.

"How's business?" He boomed.

"It's okay, I guess." Flora was a little discouraged.

Mr. Stuart stroked his bushy red beard.

"Got some tough customers, eh?"

Flora nodded. She wasn't sure that the tall man would understand how important those blue skates were for her to own.

Mr. Stuart looked at the pins once more.

"You know, sometimes when things don't sell in my shop? I go and study other places to see what I can be doing differently. Don't give up, m'girl. Just keep at it and keep that cheerful smile and you'll get far!"

Flora thanked the shop owner. Then she thought about the cork board sign outside the shop. What did that sign have that she didn't have? She shrugged and continued trying to get people to come to her table. Soon, Juniper and the whole Lucas family came over. They were at the Youth Hockey Tournament to see Mr. Lucas and Jasper play hockey. Juniper eyed the pretty bobby pins. They sparkled in the bright lights.

"Hi Flora! Those are so pretty! How do you use them?"

"Hi Juniper! These work just like regular bobby pins. But they are longer and stronger. You need to open them carefully, and pull them out slowly, because they're *so* strong."

"Wow! Cool!" Said Juniper. "How much are they? I have some spending money for cinnamon hot cocoa, but maybe I can get some bobby pins instead."

Flora smiled. "Well, it should say on the sign, silly!"

Juniper frowned. "What sign?"

30

Flora looked at her table. She frowned. She looked under the table. No sign. She reached in her pocket.

"Aha! Found it!" Flora looked at Juniper and smoothed out the paper sign. "Here we are! Bobby Pins cost $3.00 each, or you can get two bobby pins for $6.00."

Juniper grinned. "Thanks! It's so much easier to know what to buy when I can know the prices. Now I just have to choose. I really love them both so much! Can I have one gold flower pin please?"

"For sure!" Said Flora. "Thank you for your business *Miss Lucas.*"

Juniper grinned, counting out three dollars in coins from her purse and putting the pretty pin in her hair. "You're very welcome, *Miss Joy.*" Both girls giggled. "I'd love to help you at your booth if you would like." She leaned forward to whisper "I'm not a fan of ice hockey."

"Sure!" Said Flora. "That would be great. Maybe you can help me figure out why nobody else will buy from me."

The two girls worked at the booth until it was time for a dinner break. They shared hot soup and cold ham sandwiches. It was hard to remember that outside, only twenty feet away, the night air was warm with the late summer sun having just gone down. The girls talked about the blue skates and all the things that Flora might wear when she skated wearing them. Juniper had a lot of great ideas to try. She bubbled over with ideas and the girls talked and went back to the table to see if any of Juniper's suggestions might work.

First, she suggested that they get rid of the chair behind the table. "Maybe people might think we're resting if we sit down." Juniper said. She was right. When people saw the girls standing, they spent more time coming to the table to look at the pretty pins.

"I know!" said Juniper. "Let's do a *demo.*"

"That's a great idea!" said Flora. "That's actually what *Purple Lady* did when we first started our family business!"

The two girls took turns showing people how to put in the pretty pins. Soon there were more and more ladies, young and old buying pins. The girls were chatting non-stop. By the time the first night of the tournament was done, every pin was sold.

Both girls were exhausted. The ice rink was clearing out and Flora started counting out her money.

"Seventeen, eighteen, nineteen, twenty, twenty-one…" Twenty-one? Where did the rest go? There should be nine dollars more!"

Flora looked under the table. She looked inside all of her pockets. She looked under her sign. The money was nowhere. She looked at Juniper. Juniper was watching the *zamboni* in the center of the rink, it was a great, big machine used to smooth out the ice. Flora didn't like how she felt inside. She felt sad and grumpy. *What if Juniper took the money?* She thought. She could feel her face getting warm. Juniper was her friend. She didn't like to think her friend would *steal.*

Juniper turned to Flora and grinned. "Did you see that man in the *zamboni?* He's wearing a huge cowboy hat and has flipflops on!" She noticed Flora frowning. "Wait, what's wrong?"

Flora didn't know what to say. She didn't want to hurt Juniper's feelings, but there were *nine whole dollars missing.* Her throat felt like there was something stuck inside of it. She cleared her throat.

"Juniper?" she whispered. "Did you take nine dollars?"

Juniper's eyes narrowed.

"No," She frowned. "I didn't."

Flora squirmed. "Well, I have nine dollars missing. Do you know where they might be?"

Juniper frowned even more.

"No. Every time someone bought a bobby pin, I gave *you* the money."

Flora frowned. "But I don't *have* the money. Juniper.

33

So *you* must have it still." It was very logical.

Juniper crossed her arms. "I don't like what you're saying. You think I would steal from you?"

Flora could feel tears in her eyes. "I don't think you should come and help me tomorrow, Juniper." She had never felt so sad before.

Juniper nodded. Her eyes had tears in them too. "Yeah, I don't like being accused of stealing." She left in a hurry to join her family.

Flora began to put her things away. The rest of the Joy family chose that very moment to appear.

"Florrie! How did it go?" Asked Tansy. Fauna looked all over the table.

"Wow! Looks like you did good!" said Fauna.

"What's wrong? Said Zeb, chugging a sports drink. "You look like you lost your best friend."

"Mom, Dad." Flora said. "I just don't know what to do!" She burst into tears.

CHAPTER SEVEN

It was Friday Night. It had been a very rough day. Flora still didn't know what to think about the missing nine dollars. She *really* didn't think that Juniper had taken the money, but the fact was, the money was still missing.

She tried to smile and sell her bobby pins. Since the pins took a whole day to arrive in the mail, Mrs. Joy had stocked up her pin collection and had made sure that Flora was able to buy more pins from her instead of waiting to order more.

Mom and Dad had sat down with Flora and let her explain the money mix-up. They listened, asked questions, and even helped Flora search for the missing nine dollars, but nobody had found *anything.*

Then the phone had rang. It was Mrs. Lucas. She told Mr. and Mrs. Joy that Juniper was still very upset. The two moms discussed the money situation. Mrs. Lucas shared that Juniper had been sure that she had no idea where the money could be. Between the Joys and the Lucas's, *nobody* could figure out what happened. It was a rough situation.

Despite all of this, Flora was determined to keep working hard. She knew that the loss of nine dollars was not good, but she thought if she worked hard enough, that nine dollars might not matter. And she was convinced that even if Juniper *did* take the money, that she would still earn what she needed for her beautiful blue skates.

It wasn't nearly as fun working the table at the ice rink without Juniper. Tansy came and helped for a while, and Fauna came over too, but neither girl had the great ideas that Juniper had. Flora sighed. It was hard to be cheerful without Juniper to keep her company.

The bobby pins even seemed to sell slower that night. Yesterday, Flora and Juniper had sold *ten whole pins*. Today, she had been there an hour already and only sold five. She still needed to sell sixteen more pins.

The crowd was bigger tonight. This was the *playoffs* for the Youth Hockey League. That meant that more and more people would be coming to watch the men and boys play. It *should* have meant more business. But instead, everyone was focused on the game or visiting the pro shop.

Flora looked over her shoulder at the pro shop. Mr. Stuart had a huge line going out the door and she could hear his big booming voice and the sound of the skates being sharpened. She hoped he was making more money than she was.

She turned and looked away from the Pro Shop.

There was the lady in the red jumpsuit again. She was one of the figure skating coaches. Flora watched her thoughtfully. What was she doing here? She wasn't here to play hockey, probably.

The coach went up to the Community Billboard and put her sign up. It read:

Figure Skating Lessons with Coach Tasha - $140.00

Flora wanted to ask about the lessons, but she was shy all of a sudden. Besides, Coach Tasha looked too important and busy to talk to.

Soon, Flora started getting some more sales. A lady came up and bought two pins, a little girl came and bought another. Slowly, but surely, she sold all but three pins. She counted the money carefully.

"Fifty-two, fifty-three, fifty-four." She was excited. She only needed to sell nine more bobby pins to make her eighty dollars.

"Oh, hey girly!" It was Mr. Stuart.

"Hi Mr. Stuart! How are you?" Flora asked, smiling up at the burly man.

"Oh, mighty fine! Hey, I had a question- is there any chance you might have dropped some money last night?"

"Yes!" Flora was shocked. "I'm missing nine dollars!"

Mr. Stuart put his hand into his pockets.

"Well, then, it *must* be yours. It was turned in last night after the *Zamboni* was put away. I guess it was dropped on the floor near the snack shop. I was so tired myself, I just tucked it into my pocket, but when I checked my numbers this morning, I noticed I wasn't missing anything. Sorry to worry you, girlie!"

Flora was so happy. She ran up to Mr. Stuart and gave him a big bear hug.

"I was worried but I'm not anymore! Thank you so much!"

CHAPTER EIGHT

The next day, as early as her parents would allow, Flora called Juniper on the telephone to apologize and explain what happened. Juniper was happy for her friend and eager to be friends again.

"I was so upset that I even started to wonder if I *did* take the money." Juniper said. "I'm *so* glad Mr. Stuart and the *Zamboni* man found it."

"Me too!" said Flora. "Would you like to come and help me again tonight? It was *so much better* having a friend along. Tansy and Fauna are great, but it's nice to have something without sisters sometimes."

"Well, of course, silly!" Juniper said, laughing with relief. "How much more do we need to sell?"

Flora told her. "We only need to sell twelve more pins, but I can buy a lot more from Mom. What do you think?"

Juniper answered, "Look, it's the last night of the tournament, right? Let's just sell what we can. Maybe you can even get some pink hockey tape with the extra!"

"Wow! That's a great plan!" said Flora. "Let's do it!"

The two girls worked hard plotting and planning all day, preparing for the last night of their sales. Juniper really had a *knack* for sales. (Knack means something that someone is naturally good at.) In fact, every time that Flora came up with a problem, Juniper would come up with three ideas that might help to solve the problem.

"What should I do if I run out of snowflake bobbies and someone wants a snowflake bobby?" Flora asked.

"You could let them place an order." Juniper suggested. "Oh! You should make a sign to go on the Community Billboard. I think people might like to order things from you for their skating outfits or for Christmas gifts. They make pretty cool bookmarks too."

"Great ideas!" Said Flora. "I don't know what I'd do without your help. It was so *boring* last night without you. I got sales but it was so much better when we were being a team and we could work together."

"I had a lot of fun too," admitted Juniper. "And I can't wait to see those skates on you! You're gonna be able to skate even better with such pretty feet."

"I know, right?" Flora squealed. "I guess I'd better get off the phone. Mom said I could call and plan with you but the timer is going off. I've got to go and get my math done. Those times tables won't do themselves!"

"Good luck, see you tonight!" Said Juniper.

Later that night the two girls pulled out all the stops.

They sold more bobby pins than ever. They smiled and cheered, they complimented one another, anyone who passed by, and did several demonstrations. They even walked around the crowd to ask ladies if they would like to try a bobby pin or two. Each and every pin was sold before their dinner break of hot soup and ham sandwiches. Flora counted the money she had in her pocket.

"One-hundred and eighty-one, one-hundred and eighty-two, one-hundred and eighty-three, one hundred and eighty-four. Wow!"

"That's a lot of money." Said Juniper." Are we out of bobby pins?'

Flora nodded.

"Yes, we're completely out. Like, *nothing* left. I think I bought out my mom's whole supply too, so we can't ask her to go home and get more." She had never held so much money in her hands before.

"Well, you definitely have enough for some skates. You could even buy *brand new skates* with $183.00." Juniper said. Her eyes were sparkling with joy for her friend's good fortune.

"You know what? I could!" Flora said. "Since we're out of bobby pins, why don't we go get some cocoa, my treat! And let's go look around in the pro-shop again! I want to see what might be for sale in there, now that I am 'a lady of *independent means."*

They both giggled at this description (it was one that Flora's Granny Rice used to describe someone who had a lot of extra money in their pockets.) The cinnamon cocoa was wonderful but even more wonderful was that the two girls were friends again.

CHAPTER NINE

The next day was Sunday. Flora was rushing down the hallway, fast as could be. She was in a hurry again. This time, she managed to dodge the cat as she ran from Mom's office area to her room. She thumped into the door frame as she made the turn, grabbing her skate catalog and shoved it into her backpack.

Flora was excited, the whole Joy family had been invited to lunch with the Lucas family and they were going to be able to spend the day playing together. The Joys had never been to the Lucas family house, so it was a new adventure for them all. Flora was curious to see where they lived and what Juniper and Jasper's world was like.

Flora checked her bag one more time before she loaded into the van with her siblings into and made sure she had everything she needed for the day ahead.

"When did you want us to call about those ice skates?" Mr. Joy asked Flora, as they traveled into town.

"Oh, tomorrow, probably." Flora said.

"Hey! Llama!" Shouted Tansy.

"Pigs!" said Zeb.

"Squirrel!" Shouted Fauna.

"Shoes!" Giggled Flora. Sure enough, there were a

pair of shoes tied together, hanging off of a power line.

"I wonder how *those* got there?" Flora asked.

"An excellent question!" Mr. Joy replied. "Anyone want to take a guess?"

Zeb looked up at the shoes.

"They look kind of old." He said.

"Yeah, they're not the expensive kinds that you see on *Super Sports Gladiator Rock Stars."* Agreed Tansy.

The kids thought about it some more.

"Do you think…" Flora started. "this sounds terrible but maybe someone threw somebody's shoes up there? Like to be mean?"

"Well," Fauna said, "I mean, we don't know the *why.* It could have been any reason."

"Yes, that's true." Said Flora.

"I've seen shoes thrown up onto power line and phone lines as long as I can remember." Mrs. Joy said. "It always gets my attention. I always think *what's the story behind those shoes?* And you know what? I've still never figured it out."

"I guess it's a mystery!" laughed Tansy.

"It sure is." Agreed Mrs. Joy.

The rest of the trip into town continued as normal and the Joys soon settled into their classes. The lesson this

44

week was in the New Testament.

"If a man asks you to walk with him a mile, walk with him two miles." Said Mrs. Johnston.

"What does that mean? It sounds like a real mystery!" Asked Fauna, raising her hand.

"Back in those days, when a Roman soldier asked someone to help them carry their gear, they had to walk *one mile* with them, by the law of the land. In this section, Jesus is telling the people to not only do what's the law, but also to be a friend and do a whole mile more." Mrs. Johnston explained.

She continued. "Sometimes, you might hear someone say that it's a good idea to "go the extra mile." That's exactly where that saying comes from."

Flora listened to her teacher and thought about the lesson as she worked on the word puzzle that was passed out to everyone. She saw the words *good Samaritan* and circled them. She looked for more words and saw the words *friendship* and *honor.* She circled those as well.

Soon, the Sunday School bell rang, and class was dismissed. She was so excited to go to the Lucas house for lunch. Mrs. Joy had been busy that morning too, bringing all the toppings for the special lunch.

Mrs. Lucas had laughed when Mrs. Joy first

suggested *"Hawaiian Haystacks."* It was an unusual dish, but perfect for two families getting together for the first time. It included shredded chicken, on top of rice, and served with gravy. As you added all the toppings on top of the dish, it made each dinner unique. You could have it piled with fifteen fruits, vegetables, cheeses and nuts, or you could just keep the whole thing super simple and enjoy chicken, rice, and gravy. It also happened to be Flora's absolute favorite lunch. She hoped that Juniper loved it as well.

Both families pulled into the little apartment complex on Oak avenue. The Joy children had never been to an apartment before. They had read about them, certainly, and in fact, had driven by this apartment complex before, but they had never seen an apartment home up close and personal. The Lucas family had a corner apartment on the second story of a blue building.

Everyone piled out, chatting with the Lucas's, who were waiting next to their own green car.

"This is so cool!" Zeb said. "Look! They have a basketball court right over there! He grinned at Jasper. "Wanna play ball?"
Sure enough, there was a little basketball court just across from the Lucas apartment building.

"Dude! Yes!" Jasper said. "Can we play 'till lunch

Dad?"

Mr. Lucas nodded. "Sure thing boys, just listen for the bell."

"Bell?" Flora asked Juniper.

"You'll see!" Juniper said, smiling shyly.

Both families, minus the boys, climbed the steps to the apartment on the second floor. There was a little porch area, just wide enough for a gliding bench. Flora sat down immediately on the bench. You could see the whole town from there. It was pretty amazing.

Juniper sat next to her friend. She picked up a little bell that was next to the bench.

"See? Mom got tired of yelling for us to come upstairs and worried that she would wake the neighbors (some of them work late.) so Dad found this cool metal bell and we ring it when it's time to come home."

"Wow!" Said Flora. "That's really cool! Do you think I could ring it for lunch? Please?"

Juniper laughed. "Well I don't know, but we can ask. Hey, while we're waiting for lunch, can I show you my room? I just unpacked!"

CHAPTER TEN

It was Monday morning. There were waffles and hash browns for breakfast. Everyone, even Dad got up a little slowly that morning. The weekend had been very busy and a *huge* success. Not only had the boys finished up the Youth Hockey League season by winning second place, but Flora had earned almost one-hundred-and-ninety dollars with her bobby pin sales. In addition to all of this, the whole family had enjoyed a lovely time getting to know the Lucas family.

Flora had especially enjoyed seeing Juniper's bedroom. Juniper had decorated her room in purple and pink and had added large framed posters of famous figure skaters. She even had some special medals that she had put up on the walls. Some of the medals were plain and some were very fancy with shiny bits of yellow and silver.

Juniper had shown Flora photos of her skating in California. There were a lot of pictures like this. Juniper's mom had taken all the photos and put them into a special book. On the cover, there was a glittery ice skate with words next to it. The words said: "*She believed she could, so she did.*"

It was obvious that the skating world was one that

Juniper had not only been a part of in California, but that she had been good at what she did. Flora imagined her shy friend skating on the ice with a coach. She wondered why Juniper didn't have one now. She hadn't wanted to ask, it seemed like a rude question.

When she went to bed Sunday night the question still bothered her. This morning she was determined to get some answers.

"Mom?" Flora asked.

"Yes?" Mrs. Joy replied, looking away from her library book at Flora.

"Did you notice all the pretty skate things that Juniper had?"

"Yes." Mom answered. "Mr. Lucas was telling us that Juniper had been skating since she was in kindergarten. She's having a hard time adjusting to the move."

"Mom, why doesn't she get lessons here?" It seemed so simple to Flora. If Juniper loved to skate, and she had lessons in California, why not in Idaho?

Mom looked at Dad.

"The fact is that Mr. Lucas had to move here to find work. They've been making it okay, and he's got a great job now, but they haven't had the money for extras. Ice skating lessons are definitely an extra." Dad said.

49

Flora frowned. She hated to think that her friend would go without lessons because of something as silly as money.

She made up her mind.

"Mom, Dad." She started. "Do I have to buy those blue skates?"

"Have to?" Mom looked surprised. "No, I don't think you have to, but Honey, don't you want those skates?"

"Sure." Said Flora. "But you know what? I've been thinking about this. I can make money to buy things any time, right?"

Mom nodded.

"Then it's settled! Let's gift this money to help Juniper's family do lessons again, and I'll just get skates another time!"

Mr. and Mrs. Joy both smiled at one another.

Mrs. Joy raised an eyebrow at Mr. Joy.

Mr. Joy cleared his throat, walked over to Flora and gave her a big hug. Flora laughed.

"Flora-bell. That is a wonderful idea. I love the way you think." Let's call the Lucas' right away and tell them the news."

Flora grinned back. It really was better to give than to receive.

50

To receive a FREE copy of the first chapter of Book 3: "Fauna Mae & The Perfect Plan" Be sure to sign up for The Joy Series Newsletter at www.nperrine.com.

Author's Note

Flora Jean & The Money Mix-Up seemed a natural follow -up to *Tansy Joy & Too Many Tangles* to me because running a business is frankly a *huge* concept for a young person to understand.

At the end of book one, we find the Joys investing in a family business, and just as the Joys did this, so has our family.

Now, we never expected much to come out of our family side-hustle (as Dave Ramsey would call it). We just hoped it would be a fun project and that we might be able to pay a few bills off that had been lingering. In addition to the extra income, the adorable and sturdy hair accessories would be well-used in a family with no less than four daughters.

Funnily enough, our little side-gig actually took off and began to show results that were a game-changer in our family budget! It took off so quickly that soon our kids were fascinated by the idea that we could earn money by selling things.

It was immediately obvious that such a business would be an excellent learning tool. Rather than discarding their curious questions for a later time or explain it away as "adult stuff" we decided to intentionally include them from the start. Why not?

The sooner our kids could learn to use money as a tool and grasp these basic life skills, the better their success would be later on, no matter what their career choices may be. When it comes to money, In plenty or in need, there's always a life lesson to be learned.

If in fact, you are thinking you might want to join the Joys in their *Purple Lady* adventures, or that perhaps selling hair accessories might be the perfect way to introduce basic consumer economics to your own children, please consider looking into the real-life side-business offered by Lilla Rose, Inc. here on my personal business website: www.lrose.biz/alabasterjar/join

All that to be said, this book has attempted to tackle some very *real* concepts such as marketing, salesmanship, problem-solving, brainstorming, character, giving, borrowing, lending, and ethics. I hope it brings fruitful conversation to your own family table and look forward, as always, to bringing the next tale of the Joy Series into your homes.

Author Niccole Perrine

About the Author

Niccole Perrine was born in Upstate New York and raised primarily in Southern California and Southcentral Alaska. She now lives in Southwest Idaho with her husband, Luke. She is the oldest sibling out of six and mother to five children, whom she educates at home. Her favorite hobbies include reading, writing, thrift shopping, and playing tabletop games with her friends and family. She is the author of *Tansy Joy & Too Many Tangles** (Book 1 in the Joy Series)*

**#1 Amazon Bestseller Children's Books about Horses, September 2019

About the Illustrator

Teagan Ferraby is a Painter, Illustrator, and Graphic Designer. She illustrates children's books and covers, specializes in sea life paintings and has been hired for commissioned artwork. She attends The Cleveland Institute of Art where she is working towards a BFA in Graphic Design. Teagan's inspiration comes mainly from her hobbies such as scuba diving, reading, and eco dyeing. Visit https://www.facebook.com/Teagansart and https://teagan-ferraby.jimdosite.com to explore her latest works of art

Made in the USA
Monee, IL
25 August 2020